LARGE PRINT

Bedtime
Read and Count

Brown Watson

ENGLAND

Timmy the Tortoise

Timmy the tortoise had been a part of the family for as long as Joe could remember. Timmy was much older than Chips, the dog. He was even older than Joe himself.

'Your Grandad brought Timmy home when I was a boy!' Joe's dad often said. 'And he is still going strong!'

But, like all tortoises, Timmy was also very slow! While Joe and Chips raced up and down the garden, Timmy just sat on the grass, peeping out of his shell.

'Old slow-coach!' barked Chips. 'Even Horace the hamster is faster than you! Half the time Joe cannot even see you moving about in your dull shell!'

But Timmy did not mind being slow. He liked to stop and watch butterflies flying about, or a hedgehog rolling into a prickly ball, then unrolling again.

Then, one day, Joe called, 'Here, boy!'
'Mind out, Timmy!' barked Chips.
'Not you, Chips!' laughed Joe. 'It's Timmy
that I want.'

'I want to see where you are, Timmy!' said
Joe. 'So I am putting this white paint on
your shell, then everyone can find you! Isn't
that a great idea?'

Timmy was not sure that he liked wearing
white paint! But Joe looked pleased.
'Put that tortoise down, Joe!' said Mum.
'I want you to help me!'

'Grandma is coming to stay with us for a little while,' said Mum. 'She will be arriving soon!'
Joe liked Grandma!
'Coming!' he cried and ran down the path.

Chips ran after Joe and Timmy followed
Chips, slowly, as usual.
'Slow-coach!' Chips barked. 'Now we can
see just how slow you are!'

Joe and Chips ran inside, leaving Timmy in the garden. For once, he did wish he could run like Chips. After all, Chips was never left out of anything.

Timmy was still feeling sorry for himself
when Chips came out again. This time, he
was with a pretty little poodle dog.
'Fifi!' called a voice. 'Don't go too far!'

'Chips will look after Fifi!' said Joe. 'They're friends already!' But Grandma was looking at Timmy. 'That old tortoise!' she cried. 'He never changes!'

Timmy did not like the sound of that! Seeing Chips and Fifi playing together made him feel old, and very, very slow! As for Fifi, she was hardly ever still!

Fifi was always rushing around! One afternoon, she was even more fidgety than usual. 'Fifi!' cried Joe. 'Stop jumping in and out of my pool!'

But Fifi had not finished! She jumped up at
Joe's Dad, pawing at his leg and barking
all the time. Timmy was glad to stay in the
shade, out of the way!

'I think there is going to be a storm!' cried Mum. 'It has been so hot today! Bring your things inside, Joe, as quickly as you can!'

Joe just had time to put on his shirt and shorts before the rain began.
'Get everything in the shed!' yelled Dad.
'That was a flash of lightning just now!'

As they rushed indoors, there came a clap of thunder. Chips growled. Fifi started barking. Before anyone could stop her, she ran out into the storm!

'No wonder she's been so jumpy!' said Dad. 'She knew the storm was on its way!' 'Fifi!' cried Grandma. 'Come back, Fifi! Don't be frightened!'

They stood at the door, calling Fifi's name.
The storm made everywhere very dark. But
Joe could just see a splash of white moving
along very slowly...

'That's Timmy!' he cried. 'But he NEVER stays out in a thunderstorm like that!' Then Joe had an idea. 'Maybe we ought to go and see why, Grandma!'

Grandma fetched her umbrella and they went outside. The thunder and lightning had stopped, but it was still raining. 'Look!' cried Joe. 'There's Timmy!'

And as Timmy made his way slowly all the way to the end of the garden, Grandma and Joe followed. 'Fifi!' cried Grandma. 'Oh, Fifi! Where are you?'

Then, as Timmy got to the shed, they heard a tiny, little whimper. 'Fifi!' cried Grandma joyfully. 'Did the storm frighten you?' She held out her arms and Fifi jumped up.

'Fifi!' she said. 'Timmy may be old and slow, but he led the way to you! He's a clever tortoise!'
'He is!' said Joe. 'But now it will be quicker if I carry him home!'

COUNTING CLOWNS
1 to 10

Join the Counting Clowns,
And, then –
You'll soon learn
To count to ten!

One to ten

1

One dog pushes
One ball! What fun!
And, how many clowns?
That's right! There's one!

One

2

Two birds! Two rabbits!
And two clowns, too!
One drummer, one bugler –
Count them! One, two!

Two

3

Three butterflies,

Three places for tea.

Count the clowns on the
  see-saw,

There's one, two, three!

Three

4

One, two, three clowns –
And, then – one more!
How many on the boat?
One, two, three, four!

Four

5

Five fieldmice

Glad to be alive!

Counting Clowns, one
    and two,

Three, four, five!

Five

6

Six pails for jolly clowns
Practising their tricks.

Climbing high, there's one,
  two, three,

Four, five, six!

Six

7

Jumping on a trampoline,

Clowns think this is heaven!

There's one, two, three and four,

Five, six, seven!

Seven

8

Holding on to eight balloons,

Clowns in such a state!

There's one, there's two –

There's three and four,

Five, six, seven, eight!

Eight

9

Clowns now climbing up a tree,

And everything is fine!

There's one, there's two, three,
  and four –

Five, six, seven, eight, nine!

Nine

10

Clowns are altogether, now –

So, count them once again!

One, two, three, four, five, six, seven –

Eight, nine, ten!

Ten

1 to 10

One Counting Clown says,
  "Goodbye

But please come back again!

We'll have such fun every time

That we count up to ten!"

One to ten

Lady and Rover

Every day, Rover, the sheep-dog at Buttercup Farm, waited at the gate to see his friend, Lady. She was a splendid white poodle, with a smart collar and a ribbon bow tied on top of her head. Lady lived in a big white house at the end of the lane.

As soon as Rover saw Lady, his tail began to wag and he gave a friendly bark. 'Woof! Hello, Lady! I have been waiting for you!' Lady was always pleased to see Rover.

Sooner or later, there always came a sharp voice. 'Lady! Come here! You will get your feet wet!' Or – 'Just look at your lovely, woolly coat! It is COVERED in mud!'

Really, Lady only had a few splashes of mud. But Miss Fox, the lady she lived with, was always fussing about her dog. She did not like Lady getting in a mess!

Rover was looking forward to seeing Lady in the big parade at the Dog Show! With her ribbons and pretty bows, he was sure she would win first prize!

And Rover? He was going to be in the Sheep-Dog Competition, showing everyone how well he could round up sheep and put them safely into the pen.

Tim, the shepherd, had trained Rover since he was a puppy. He only had to use his whistle and Rover knew what to do. It was a special whistle that only dogs can hear.

As the day of the Dog Show got nearer, the more Lady was brushed and groomed and fussed over. 'You are sure to win first prize!' smiled Miss Fox. 'I shall be SO proud of you!'

Even on the day of the Dog Show, Miss Fox
kept brushing Lady's coat and polishing her
little claws. Lady did not like it very much.
She wanted to see her friend, Rover.

Soon it was time for Lady and Miss Fox to parade in the show ring. 'Hold your head up high, Lady!' said Miss Fox. 'Let the judges see what a pretty dog you are!'

People who were watching began to clap.
'What a lovely dog!' said one lady to her
friend. 'I do hope the judges choose her.
She deserves to win the prize!'

And in another field, Rover was also doing well! He had rounded up a flock of sheep and got them all together. Now all he had to do was to get them into the pen.

Tim blew his whistle as a signal for Rover. But, in the show ring, Lady heard it too! She knew that sound very well! It was Tim whistling for Rover!

Miss Fox felt Lady pulling at her lead.
'Stop, Lady!' she cried. 'Be a good girl!'
Tim blew his whistle again. This time, Lady
gave a loud bark. She tugged at her lead
more strongly.

Then Lady stood on her back legs and
pawed at the air. That was the sound of
Rover's whistle! Miss Fox could not hear it,
but Lady could! She knew that her friend
was somewhere near.

'Stop, Lady!' cried poor Miss Fox. But it was
no good. Lady pulled so hard at her lead,
she pulled Miss Fox over, right into the mud!
'Oh, no!' she moaned. 'My lovely, new suit!'

But that was not all. Lady was running into the next field, mud and clumps of grass flying everywhere! She looked around for Rover, but all she could see was a whole lot of sheep!

Lady ran around the sheep, first one way,
and then the other, just as she had watched
Rover doing. Before long, she had got all
the sheep into a tidy little group.

'Oh, no!' cried Miss Fox again, so loudly that everyone could hear. 'Just look at my beautiful poodle, Lady! She is dirty, she is muddy, she is untidy, she – she ...'

'She has just rounded up all those sheep and got them safely into the pen!' said Tim with a grin. 'Without anyone training her, too! What a clever dog she is!'

'Winner of the beginner class in the Sheep-Dog Competition!' boomed the voice of a judge. 'But I do not have the name of this poodle! What is she called? Who does she belong to?'

'She belongs to me!' cried Miss Fox. Now, she sounded very proud indeed! 'And her name is Lady!'

Then everyone began clapping and cheering all over again.

Tim led Rover across to see Lady. The two friends rubbed noses and wagged their tails. They were both so pleased to win a prize! As for Tim and Miss Fox, they started talking.

Lady is still a splendid white poodle, with pretty ribbons and a bow on top of her head. And Rover is still a hard-working sheep-dog with mud on his paws.